For Emma, Elsie and Emile - M.R.
For baby Scout. Welcome to the World. - M.F.

First published 2012 by Walker Books Ltd
87 Vauxhall Walk, London SE11 5HJ

This edition published 2012

10 9 8 7 6 5 4 3 2 1

This book has been typeset in Stempel Schneidler

Printed in China

British Library Cataloguing in Publication Data:
a catalogue record for this book is available from
the British Library

ISBN 978-1-4063-4437-0

www.walker.co.uk

Michael Rosen
BLUE

illustrated by
Michael Foreman

WALKER BOOKS
AND SUBSIDIARIES

LONDON • BOSTON • SYDNEY • AUCKLAND

Raffi's big brother Jake could run very fast, jump very high, sing, dance and draw elephants.

Raffi looked at Jake. "You're good at everything, aren't you, Jake?"

"Yep," said Jake.

I wish I was good at something, thought Raffi.

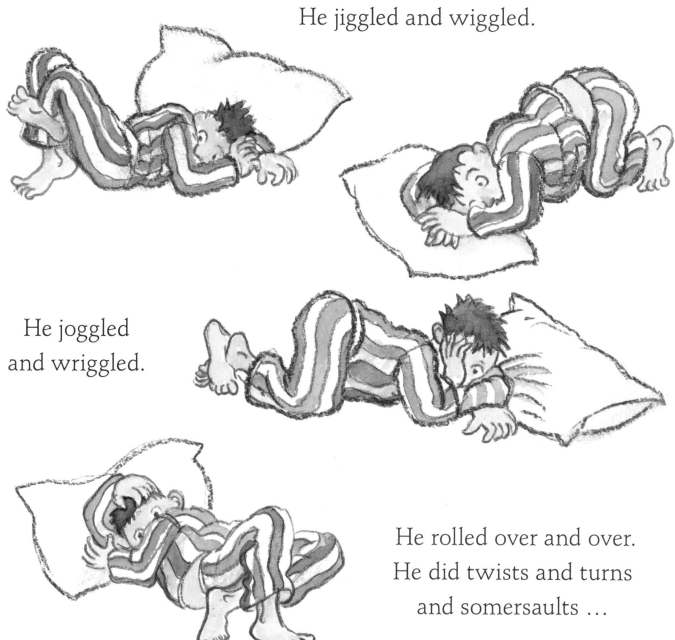

At bedtime, Raffi couldn't sleep.
He jiggled and wiggled.

He joggled
and wriggled.

He rolled over and over.
He did twists and turns
and somersaults …

till his feet lay on the pillow and his
head was where his feet used to be.

Wow! It was
dark. Totally dark.
Darker than dark.

Dark is good,
Raffi thought.
No one knows
I'm here. Maybe
I don't know
I'm here.

Then, far off, he saw a tiny
blue light. He reached out
for it and a voice said,
"Are you Raffi the Jiggler
Raffi the Wiggler
Raffi the Joggler
Raffi the Wriggler?"

"That's me," said Raffi. "Who are you?"

"I'm Blue," said the voice.
"And you're just the person
I need. Follow me."

And Blue headed off deep into the dark.

Raffi felt himself flying along after. He could see now that Blue was…

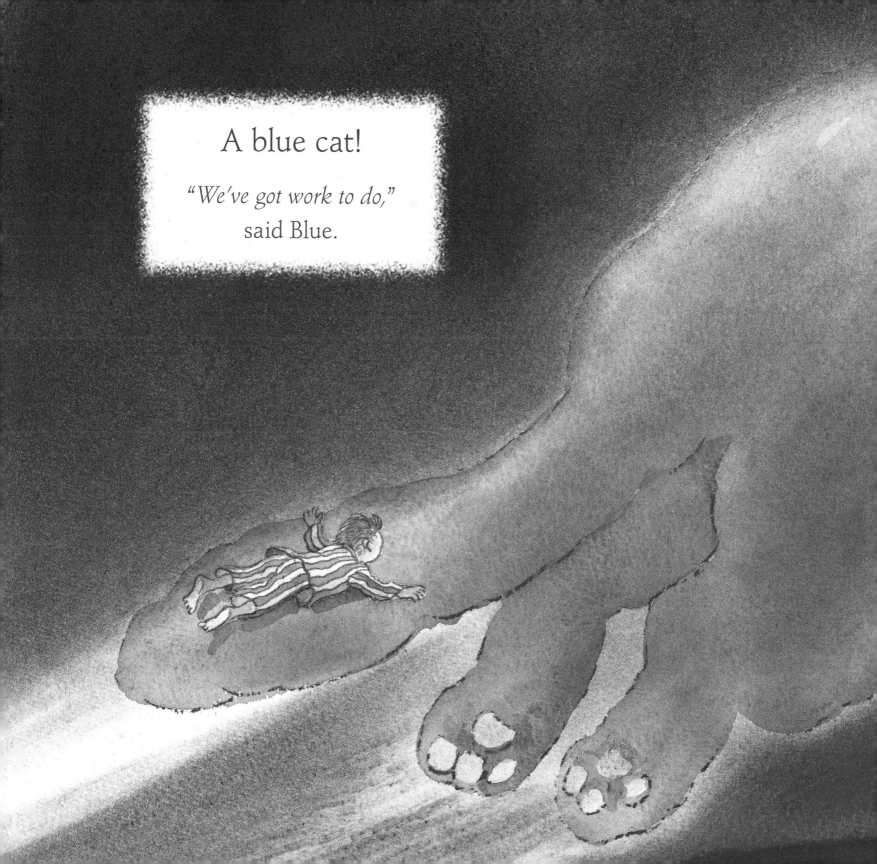

A blue cat!

"*We've got work to do,*"
said Blue.

Dipping and swooping, Blue and Raffi flew towards the signs over shops and stores. The moment Blue touched them, they lit up.

Blue and Raffi glided across to the cinema and lit up the cinema sign …

then over to the railway, and Blue threw sparks behind the electric train. Each time Blue pointed at something, there was a pop and a blue light flicked on.

"*Blue light,*" said Blue, "*but not light blue.*"

I like that, thought Raffi, blue light, but not light blue.

On and on and on they flew. "Where now?" asked Raffi.

"*Hold tight,*" said Blue and they swooshed up, up, up…

And pop! on came the stars.

"Oh wow!" said Raffi. "But where does all the blue come from?"

"Every jiggle and wiggle you do
Every joggle and wriggle you do
Gives me the power to make
things blue," said Blue.
"That's power. Pow!"

"Pow!" said Raffi.

Down they swooped,   down, down, down,   towards the city,

towards Raffi's home,   towards Raffi's room,   towards Raffi's bed.

Back in his bed, Raffi was looking
and looking at his blue light.

Am I looking at the light? Or is the
light looking at me? he wondered.

In the morning Raffi ate his breakfast,
while Jake drew elephants.

That night, they walked home from school.

"Hurry, Raffi," said Jake. "Let's get home before dark."

"It's OK," said Raffi, looking at the cinema sign flicking on.
"See that? *Blue light. But not light blue.*"

"Wow!" said Jake, and he smiled. "I like that.
Blue light, but not light blue."

Together they walked
down the street with Jake saying,
"Blue light," and Raffi saying,
"but not light blue."

And pop! the sky lit up with stars.